My
with Birds

Henrietta Higgins

Written by Jill Eggleton
Illustrated by Philip Webb

MY SHOE SHOP DAYS

I was born in Brinwick. My parents owned a shoe shop. I was their only child and so I had to learn to entertain myself.

When I was little, my parents took me to the shoe shop every day. I hated the shoe shop. I hated being inside all day and I hated people coming in for my mother and father to fuss about their feet.

As I got older, I thought up ways to make my time in the shoe shop more interesting. One day I pulled the laces out of all the shoes and tied them together to make a jump rope. Another time, I found a slimy slug and put it in a shoe. I loved it when a woman dressed up in fancy clothes tried the shoe on. She screamed so loud that people came running from everywhere. They thought there had been a murder in my parents' shoe shop. My parents were very angry with me. They said they had lost their best customer.

DAYS WITH MY AUNT

After I put the slug in the shoe, my parents decided I couldn't come to the shop any more. I was sent to stay with my aunt. I liked it a lot at my aunt's place because she had a big yard and I could play outside. I was worried, though, that my aunt kept birds in cages. I had decided I liked birds. I would sit in my aunt's yard and watch them for hours. I felt sorry for the birds in their cages. I had never heard them sing like birds that were free. One day I lifted the latch on their cage door and they flew away. My aunt was very upset and blamed the cat. She said she had seen it with its paw on the latch.

My aunt got some more birds, but I let them out, too. She blamed the cat again, but I think she might have changed her mind when I became a "birdwoman."

SCHOOL DAYS

When I was six years old, my father and mother separated. I stayed with my mother during the week and went to my father's place on the weekends. It was about this age that I found out birds liked me as much as I liked them. I would feed them crumbs and they would perch on my shoulders and head. I carried crumbs in my pocket so wherever I went I could feed the birds. I always had a flock of birds following me.

One day at school, a bird flew in the window and sat on my head. The teacher tried to shoo it out, but it kept coming back to sit on my head. I had to take it out and shut the window. But it knocked on the window with its beak. The kids kept laughing, so I had to do my work outside with the birds.

After that, the principal said I was not to feed the birds on the way to school.

THE BIRD PARADISE

At school I wasn't very good at mathematics, but I knew everything about birds. At home, I turned the backyard into a bird paradise. I made birdbaths and a pond. I made a large feeding table and one day I found a bald eagle on it. Birds came from everywhere. They made nests in the trees and I helped to care for the babies. My mother got a bit annoyed about all the birds in the backyard. She said every time she took the washing in there were bird droppings on it. She got tired of people knocking on the door, asking to see the birds — especially when I decided to have tours of my bird paradise. I put a sign on the gate:

BIRD PARADISE
Conducted Tours
$3.00

BIRDWATCHING IN THE AMAZON

When I left school, I had quite a lot of money saved from giving tours around my bird paradise. I decided to use the money for a jungle tour. I spent six weeks in the jungle, living in a houseboat and sometimes in tree huts. I had to wear a camouflage suit, which was extremely hot. I had special glasses made for birdwatching. It was very interesting to watch birds in the wild. I learned a lot about birds during this six weeks, and the information has been very useful to me.

BIRD TROUBLE

When I came back from the jungle, I had to find a place to live. My mother didn't want me to come back and live with her. All the birds had left when I went away and she liked it better without them. I didn't have much money and I knew I had to get a job. I found a house in the country to live in. It had plenty of room for birds and I got a job picking apples. But that job only lasted a week. Birds came with me and pecked holes in the apples. The manager said he never had trouble with birds until I arrived.

"I'm sorry," he said, "but you will have to find a new job."

The next job I got was cleaning a huge house. That job didn't last long either. The birds came and perched on the roof and left a huge mess everywhere. The owner said I would have to go and take the birds with me.

I tried all sorts of jobs, but I always seemed to have the same problem. That was when I decided to become a "birdwoman."

SETTING UP MY BIRD HOSPITAL

I went to see an old man who had lived with birds all his life.
I had never seen so many birds, even in the jungle. He told me
that he used to have a bird hospital and rescued hurt and sick
birds. Now he just had an "open house" and birds come and go
whenever they like.

I decided that I would make a bird hospital in my old house and
rescue birds that were in danger.

It took me one year to get my bird hospital ready. I had to make
all the bird beds for the sick birds and turn all my bedrooms into
bedcages for birds who were sick. When the bird hospital was
ready, I put advertisements in the newspapers and store windows.

The first job I got was to find some prize parrots that had escaped from a cage. I found them huddled under an old sack. I told their owner that there were better places than cages to keep birds. I helped her make a huge outdoor pen and trained the parrots to go in and out.

I have been very lucky with my jobs. I have been to some very interesting places. I have climbed icy mountains in the middle of winter to rescue birds. I have dangled from helicopters rescuing birds off high cliffs. I have paddled down rivers to rescue baby birds trapped by crocodiles. Once I had to travel thousands of miles to rescue a pigeon that had lost its way. I was on a tiny island. There was a terrible storm and I couldn't get off the island for a week.

I love my life with birds. Nearly every day there is some new and exciting adventure.

Autobiography

An autobiography is a story of a person's life written by the person themselves.

How to Write an Autobiography

Step One

Think of the important things you want to put in your autobiography.
Make a word web to help you brainstorm ideas.

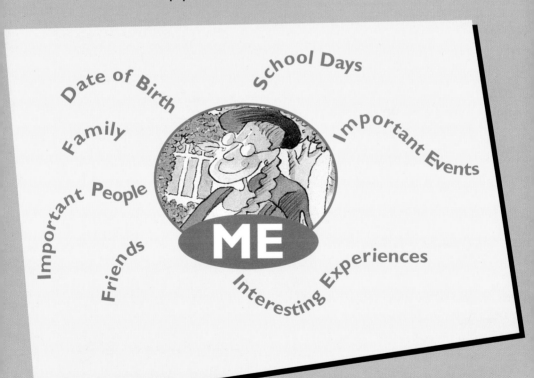

Step Two

Make a list of chapter headings to help organize the sequence of events in your life.

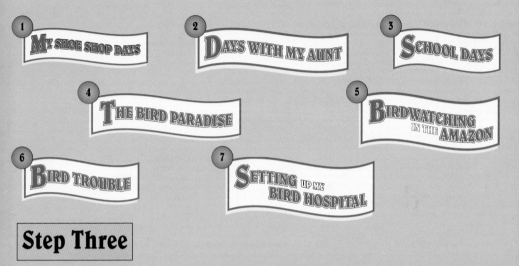

1. MY SHOE SHOP DAYS
2. DAYS WITH MY AUNT
3. SCHOOL DAYS
4. THE BIRD PARADISE
5. BIRDWATCHING IN THE AMAZON
6. BIRD TROUBLE
7. SETTING UP MY BIRD HOSPITAL

Step Three

Now use your word web and chapter headings to write your autobiography.

Step Four

Check your autobiography.
Can you add anything to make it more interesting?

Can you use artwork, photographs, letters...?

Can you take anything out that is not important in your autobiography?
Is your autobiography a true story about your life?

▬▬▬ Guide Notes

Title: My Life with Birds
Stage: Fluency (3)

Text Form: Autobiography
Approach: Guided Reading
Processes: Thinking Critically, Exploring Language, Processing Information
Written and Visual Focus: Chapter Book Layout

THINKING CRITICALLY
(sample questions)
- Why do you think Henrietta Higgins wanted to write about her life?
- What do you think are the most important things she wrote about herself?
- What sort of things could you say about Henrietta Higgins' character?
- What do you think could happen with Henrietta's book about herself?

EXPLORING LANGUAGE

Terminology
Spread, author, illustrator, credits, imprint information, ISBN number

Vocabulary
Clarify: entertain, paradise, camouflage, huddled
Pronouns: my, their, they, she
Adjectives: *slimy* slug, *huge* house, *icy* mountains
Homonyms: their/there, shoe/shoo
Antonym: separated/together
Synonym: annoyed/angry

Print Conventions
Dash, apostrophe – possessive (parents' shoe shop)